# LOVE YOU A LITTLE MORE

ANGLEBERT R. PACHECO

To my parents, who gave me the gift of dreams and the
ability to realize them.

To those rare, beautiful friendships that change our lives
forever.

For the music that scored the writing of this novel.

For all the yesterdays that led me to today

To tomorrow, for it holds unspoken stories.

For the person I was when I started writing this book, and
the person I am now.

# Contents

# PREFACE

Love has a way of shaping our lives in the most unexpected ways. It can be found in the quiet moments, in the stolen glances, and in the life-changing decisions we make. This story is one of love, courage, and the beauty of saying yes to the unknown.

As I stood beside Emily that evening, watching the sky transform into a canvas of stars, I realized that some moments are meant to be etched in time. That night, with a trembling heart and unwavering certainty, I asked her to be my wife. In her tear-filled eyes, I saw the promise of forever.

This is more than just a story about a proposal—it's a journey of love, hope, and the moments that define who we are.

# Acknowledgements

"I would like to express my gratitude to my friend Edmer Barreto, who is a published author and a teacher. He has always been there for me, guiding me through difficult times, especially when I was confused about certain topics about my book. Whenever I reached out to him, he provided me with the necessary guidance and support."

૪૭

Notion Press was instrumental in guiding me through the self-publishing process, from cover design to interior layout.

૪૭

Once again thank you to all DIL SE...(from Heart)

# Prologue

Love and pain are two sides of the same coin, forever entwined in an unbreakable dance. To love is to open yourself to the possibility of heartbreak, to risk the unbearable weight of loss for the fleeting beauty of connection. It is the most powerful force we know—capable of building worlds and tearing them apart in a single breath.

Love begins as a spark, igniting the soul with warmth and wonder. It fills the quiet spaces of our hearts, turning ordinary moments into something sacred. A touch, a glance, a whispered promise—each one carving itself into the fabric of our existence. We give ourselves to it willingly, believing in forever, hoping that what we hold is strong enough to withstand the passage of time.

But love is not without its price. With every moment of joy, there lingers the shadow of loss. Pain arrives uninvited, sometimes slowly, like a creeping tide, and other times all at once, like a storm that leaves devastation in its wake. It reminds us that nothing lasts forever, that even the strongest hearts can break.

And yet, we love. Despite the risk, despite the pain, we love. Because even in the wreckage, even in the sorrow, love is the only thing that remains. It shapes us, teaches us, and gives us something worth holding onto—even when everything else fades away.

This is a story of love and pain, of beauty and loss, of the moments that define us and the scars that remain. It is a testament to the truth that love, no matter how fleeting, is always worth it.

40

# I

# Crush on you!

Archer was the kind of person who lived in his own world. He had always been a daydreamer, his mind frequently wandering to far-off places and imaginary adventures. He found comfort in the quiet, the calm, and the beauty of his small town--a place where the gentle rustling of leaves and the distant call of birds were all that accompanied his thoughts. Though he didn't have many friends, the ones he had were his world. They were there for him through thick and thin, sharing laughs, quiet moments, and sometimes even the loudest, most reckless fun. And that night, as the warmth of a spring evening wrapped itself around them, Archer found himself in the middle of something exciting.

It all started with a simple gathering at his place. Archer had always enjoyed being the host, and tonight was no exception. The group sat around the table, sipping on drinks Archer had made using urrak, a local Goan alcohol extracted from cashew fruit. It wasn't the first time they had enjoyed the drink, but tonight felt different. The evening had that electric energy to it--the kind that makes you feel alive, makes you forget the usual worries, and encourages you to open up and say things you might not usually share.

The conversation flowed easily at first, but soon it veered into more personal territory. As the alcohol kicked in, Archer felt a mix of warmth and nervousness. His friends, being the playful bunch they were, started teasing him about something he had tried to keep hidden.

"Archer, you've got a crush on someone, don't you?" Sybil grinned knowingly, nudging him with her elbow.

Archer's cheeks flushed, his heart skipped a beat. He was caught. He tried to deny it, but the teasing only got worse. His friends laughed and even gave it a name--#ARCHERLY. The hashtag made him blush even more, his mind racing. How could they know? It was Emily, of course--Emily, the girl he had never met but couldn't stop thinking about. The girl that Sybil had introduced to him weeks earlier.

Sybil, ever the schemer, smiled and said, "You know, Emily is cute. I'll set you up with her."

The words stung Archer in the best way possible. Could it really happen? He could hardly believe it. For years, he had kept his feelings for Emily buried deep inside, never daring to admit to himself that he wanted to know her, wanted to be more than just a guy who fantasized about someone he didn't know. But tonight, something changed. Maybe it was the drinks, or maybe it was the warmth of his friends surrounding him, but for the first time, Archer felt a glimmer of hope. Perhaps, just perhaps, he could make it happen.

With a smile, he nodded at Sybil. "You'll set it up?"

"Of course," she replied confidently, "But don't get your hopes up. You'll have to wait until after Easter."

Archer's heart fluttered. That was the beginning. Little did he know, the story of Emily wasn't something that would unfold easily. It would take time, patience, and a few twists and turns before they would meet. But before any of that happened, Archer would need to look back on the few weeks that had led him to this moment.

It had all started a week before that night. Archer had been at his friend's restaurant, playing cards with the usual group of friends. Sybil, ever the conversationalist, had asked him about his feelings. "So, what does a girl look like to you? What kind of girl do you like?"

Archer had answered casually, "kind by heart and loving by nature, but why do you ask?"

Sybil had paused, looking thoughtful for a moment. "You've been single for so long, maybe it's time you found someone. I have a friend, Emily, who's also been through a rough time with her past relationship. She's great."

That was all Archer needed. He hadn't met Emily yet, but the mere thought of her had sparked something in him. As the days passed, he couldn't stop thinking about her. Who was she? What did she look like? Did she like the same things he did? The anticipation ate at him, and all he could do was check his phone, hoping for a message from Sybil, giving him a little hint about Emily.

Weeks passed. Archer had become a little obsessed. And then, finally, Sybil messaged him. His heart raced as he opened the text: "I talked to Emily. She's not looking to date right now, but I'll talk to her after Easter. Don't lose hope, okay?"

Archer sighed, disheartened, but Sybil's words lifted him up again. After Easter. That small detail gave him something to hold onto, something to look forward to.

And so, life went on, leading them all to the eagerly awaited trip to Kerala. Archer's friends had been planning this for months, and it was now only a day away. It was supposed to be a trip to explore the beautiful backwaters, lush forests, and pristine beaches of Kerala. Archer couldn't wait, but there was something else on his mind: Emily. Every thought seemed to circle back to her, and now, this trip felt like the perfect distraction, or perhaps even a chance to finally meet her.

Before the trip, one evening, Archer received a text from his friend Shawn. "Buddy... where are you???" Archer responded quickly, "I'm at home. Tell me. Shawn, in his usual humorous fashion, responded to meet Archer at a trendy restaurant in town called Hotspot. Archer, always up for a change in scenery, agreed and headed out.

Hotspot was everything the rumors had said. The atmosphere was vibrant, modern, and bustling with energy. Archer met Shawn by the window, and after some small talk, they ordered soup and French fries, enjoying a leisurely meal together. The evening was casual but refreshing--a nice break from the intensity of the last few days of preparations for the trip.

Afterward, they walked back to their respective homes, chatting about the upcoming trip and laughing about anything and everything. Archer couldn't stop smiling. For the first time in weeks, he felt relaxed and content.

The day before the trip was a whirlwind of activity. Archer and his friends went shopping to prepare for the journey. From clothes to snacks, they ensured they had everything they needed. As they made their way home, Archer suddenly realized that he had yet to pack his own bags. Panic set in, but he quickly rushed home, gathered his things, and made sure he was ready for what was sure to be an unforgettable adventure.

Later that night, they attended a midnight Easter mass, a tradition that had brought the group of friends closer over the years. At 3 AM, with Easter wishes exchanged and spirits lifted, they made their way back home. Archer changed into his travel clothes and gathered his bags, knowing the next few days would be filled with excitement, discovery, and maybe, just maybe, the chance to meet Emily.

And so, with bags packed and hearts full of anticipation, they set off toward the station, their laughter and chatter ringing in the air. It was the beginning of an adventure-- a journey that would lead Archer to discover not just the beauty of Kerala, but perhaps something deeper within himself.

The countdown to the trip had begun. It was finally time.

# II
# Kerala

It was 4:45 AM when we finally arrived at the station, the remnants of our long journey from our hometown still hanging in the air. The cool morning breeze felt refreshing, but our bodies, sore and tired from the overnight travel, craved nothing more than a soft bed. We hurried to the platform, convinced we had missed our train, but to our relief, we discovered it wouldn't be arriving until 6:00 AM. This gave us more than enough time to settle in and prepare for the next leg of our journey.

As the minutes ticked by, the station slowly began to stir to life, and we anxiously awaited the arrival of the train. The anticipation buzzed in the air, and as soon as we saw the train approaching in the distance, a collective sigh of relief swept through our group. We hurried to board, finding our seats and settling in for what was going to be a long 13-hour journey. Despite the early start, excitement bubbled within us as we thought of the adventure ahead.

As the train chugged along, we passed the hours with conversation, laughter, and games. We shared our plans for the trip—where we would go, what we would see, and of course, the delicious food we couldn't wait to try. We reminisced about old memories, and it was as if time was moving faster in the comfort of good company.

We snacked, laughed, and occasionally dozed off for short naps, knowing that the real excitement awaited when we arrived in Kerala. Finally, after what seemed like an eternity, the train pulled into the station, and we were ready to begin our exploration.

After a short cab ride from the station, we reached our motel. Varun's parents were kind enough to take us to our rooms, and we freshened up quickly. They had invited us for dinner, and we couldn't wait to experience the authentic Kerala cuisine we had heard so much about. The dishes they served were beyond delicious, with the highlight being the chicken tandoori, which was cooked to perfection. The spices, the tender meat, the smoky aroma—it was unlike anything we had tasted before. We savored every bite.

Later that evening, after thanking Varun's mom for the incredible meal, we took a leisurely walk back to our rooms, chatting about the day and what we planned to do the following morning. We had barely arrived in Kerala, and already, we were in love with the place. The excitement was palpable.

The next morning, we woke up to the reality that the night had not been as peaceful as we had hoped. The heat was stifling, and the slow-moving fan did little to cool us down. So, we decided to change rooms to one with air conditioning. The room manager was accommodating, and soon we were in a much cooler, more comfortable space. After some rest, we made our way to the hotel's restaurant for a delicious Kerala breakfast. The variety of dishes was astounding, and we made sure to try as much as we could.

With our bellies full and our spirits high, we rented bikes for the rest of our stay. The fresh air as we rode through the streets of the city was exhilarating, and we quickly found ourselves exploring new spots we hadn't planned for. We took the metro to the mall, parked our bikes, and spent the afternoon wandering through the shops, enjoying the sights, and treating ourselves to KFC for lunch. Afterward, we headed to the gaming zone, where we played several games, laughing and letting go of the day's worries. I even got lost in a bookstore, completely engrossed in a novel I found on the second floor. It was a perfect escape, and I bought the book right away.

Later, we visited a beautiful church, taking in its intricate architecture and capturing memories with photographs. We walked around the church grounds, enjoying the peace and serenity before returning to our motel via the scenic route. The natural beauty of the surroundings made the day feel even more magical, and we ended the evening by reflecting on how perfect everything had been so far.

The next day dawned with brilliant sunlight, and after a restful sleep, we were ready for more adventures. We were particularly excited about meeting Varun's cousin for lunch. Their warm hospitality and the promise of more incredible food had us eager to experience it all. When we arrived, Aunty greeted us with refreshing cold drinks and immediately made us feel at home. The biryani they had prepared was nothing short of spectacular. It was rich in flavor, with perfectly balanced spices and tender meat that melted in our mouths. We were so engrossed in the food and conversation that we almost forgot to leave.

After lunch, we decided to visit a nearby beach, a short trip that would offer a much-needed respite from the heat.

The beach was everything we had hoped for—crystal-clear waters, soft sand, and a gentle breeze. We played football, took countless pictures, and watched the sunset, mesmerized by the colors that painted the sky in shades of orange, pink, and purple. It was the perfect way to spend the afternoon.

Later that evening, we returned to our motel, freshened up, and packed for the much-anticipated bike ride the next day. We couldn't wait to explore even more of Kerala, and with the night's peaceful rest, we were ready for the adventure ahead.

The next day arrived with a promise of excitement as we embarked on a long 4-hour bike ride, a journey we had been planning for weeks. The weather was perfect, the sun shining bright, and the wind cool and refreshing. We cruised along winding roads, passing through picturesque landscapes and small villages. Every stop we made was an opportunity to snap photos, grab snacks, and bond over shared experiences.

After a brief rest at the ghats with Maggi and tea, we pushed on, our spirits high despite the exhausting journey. When we finally reached Munnar, the beauty of the place took our breath away. Lush tea plantations, rolling hills, and a cool breeze greeted us as we explored the city. We found a place to stay for the night, but unfortunately, Varun wasn't feeling well due to the climate, so he decided to go to a lower altitude to recover. We were worried, but we knew he would be okay.

The next day was filled with more exploration—tea factories, nature walks, and enjoying the delicious local cuisine. We were having the time of our lives, and each new experience brought us closer together. We knew that these were the moments we would cherish forever.

Finally, on our last day in Kerala, we decided to make it a day to remember. We hopped on the Water Metro, an eco-friendly way to explore the backwaters. The journey was peaceful, and the sights were incredible. Later, we wandered through the bustling local markets, bargaining for souvenirs and sampling street food. We even tried the famous Kerala veg thali, a flavor explosion that left us wanting more.

After all that excitement, we ventured back to our motel to change into adventure clothes, ready for a kayaking trip through Kerala's serene backwaters. The sunset was nothing short of magical as we paddled through crystal-clear waters, surrounded by nature's beauty.

As the night drew to a close, we visited Rahul's place for dinner, where we shared stories of our adventures, knowing that these memories would stay with us forever. Kerala had captured our hearts, and we couldn't help but promise to return one day, to explore more, experience more, and live life to the fullest.

This trip had been more than just a vacation—it had been an unforgettable journey filled with laughter, new experiences, and cherished memories that we would carry with us for years to come.

# III
# Friends first?

Sybil hadn't seen Emily in almost three weeks, and I asked her when they would be able to see each other again. Sybil kindly told me to be patient and said that she would be meeting with Emily the next day. I was excited to hear her response but also a little anxious. I couldn't stop thinking about what she would say and it kept me up all night.

The next day, Sybil finally met Emily and asked how she was doing. After catching up, Sybil suggested that Emily should date her friend Archer, who she described as both cute and loving. Emily was hesitant and shared her concerns about past relationships where she had been cheated on or taken advantage of. Sybil listened patiently and empathized with Emily's experiences. She encouraged Emily to give Archer a chance, saying that she had known him for a long time and was certain that he would keep her happy.

Emily was intrigued but still uncertain. Sybil could tell that Emily needed more time to think about it. She suggested that they start as friends and see where things go from there. Emily agreed, and they planned to hang out with Archer and see how they got along.

A few days later, Sybil, Emily, and Archer decided to meet at a coffee shop. As Sybil and I entered, I asked her where Emily was. Sybil replied that Emily works here and we should wait for her at the corner table.

While I was reading a book, Sybil kicked me under the table and said that Emily was coming. I looked up and saw her walking towards us in slow motion, just like in the movies. She had slightly curly hair and worn tiny earrings. I couldn't believe my eyes; I finally saw her in person. While I kept staring at her, Sybil kicked me again and said snap out of it. Emily was standing right in front of me. I stood up, shook hands, and introduced myself, and she did the same.

I was so nervous that I didn't know what to say, so we sat awkwardly for a while until Emily asked if I had tried their famous hot chocolate. I said no, and she suggested we order it. As it arrived, I took a sip, and it was indeed very tasty. Emily asked me what I do for a living and who I live with. I told her that I am currently waiting for my job confirmation and live with my parents.

I asked if she was doing part-time or if this was her fixed job, and she replied that she does part-time and is currently pursuing her masters. We talked about our interests, ambitions, and hobbies. I found that we had a lot in common and enjoyed listening to her speak. Her voice was so soothing and calming, and every word she spoke was like music to my ears.

As time went by, we talked and laughed, and Emily found herself enjoying my company. Sybil could see that we were getting along well and was thrilled. Sybil suggested that we visit the nearby park, and we all agreed. We walked to the park and talked about life, nature, and the beauty of the surroundings.

As the sun began to set, we decided to end our day together. We said our goodbyes and walked away, each lost in our thoughts.

As I walked home, I felt a sense of happiness and contentment that I hadn't felt in a long time. I knew that I had made a new friend, and I couldn't wait to see her again.

As soon as I stepped into my house, I realized that I had forgotten to exchange phone numbers with Emily. It suddenly dawned on me that I might not be able to contact her again, and I didn't want that to happen. So, I quickly messaged Sybil and asked if she could give me Emily's phone number.

To my surprise, Sybil told me that I should ask Emily directly. But, I didn't know how to approach her. That's when Sybil suggested that I could find her on social media. She gave me Emily's social media profile, and I quickly searched for her online.

When I found Emily, I noticed that she had only one profile picture and nothing else in her feed. I hesitated for a moment, wondering if it was the right thing to do, but then I decided to send her a friend request. I waited for her response anxiously.

After some time, I received a notification that Emily had accepted my friend request. I felt relieved and excited at the same time. That day, we started chatting and before I knew it, we had talked the whole night.

It's amazing how social media can help connect people who might not have met otherwise. I'm glad I took the initiative to find Emily's profile and connect with her.

Every day, I looked forward to sitting down to chat with her. She was someone who made me feel comfortable and at ease. As we caught up with each other, we would share stories about our day, our friends, and our families. Our conversations were always filled with warmth and sincerity, and I cherished every moment spent talking to her.

We would talk about everything under the sun – our dreams, aspirations, fears, and worries. There was never a topic that was off-limits, and I always felt like I could be myself around her. No matter what was going on in our lives, we would always find a way to uplift each other, to inspire and motivate each other to keep pushing forward.

Sometimes we would go out together, watch movies or just sit at the beach staring at the sunset. Those moments were special, and I treasured them all. The way the sun would dip behind the horizon, casting a warm golden light over everything around us, was a sight to behold. We would sit there in silence, taking in the breathtaking view, lost in our own thoughts.

As the day would come to an end, we would say our goodbyes and go our separate ways. But the memories of our conversations and the time we spent together would stay with me long after we parted. I knew that no matter what life threw my way, I had someone I could count on to be there for me, to support me, and to make me feel loved.

During the summer season, one day, Emily and I decided to spend our time at the mall playing games and having fun. After the games were over, we were both tired and looking for something else to do. I suggested to Emily that we watch a newly released horror movie. She replied saying that she was afraid of horror movies and only enjoyed action and romantic comedies. I encouraged her by saying that I was with her and she would not get scared.

After a bit of convincing, Emily finally agreed and we booked our tickets. As we entered the theater, we saw that it was packed to capacity. We found our seats in the middle row and settled in to enjoy the movie. As the movie began, I could sense that Emily was getting nervous. I reassured her that she was safe and that she could rely on me.

While watching the movie, during a particularly scary scene, Emily screamed loudly and held my hand tight. Actually, even I got a little scared when that scene appeared on the big screen. I felt happy as she was holding my hand, but suddenly she felt awkward and left my hand. She kept silent until the movie ended.

After the movie, I asked Emily if she would like to go and have some ice cream. She replied saying, "Why not? It's my favorite." We went to the ice cream parlor and ordered our favorite flavors. As we sat and enjoyed our ice cream, I asked Emily if she had enjoyed the movie. She said that although it was scary, she was glad she had watched it with me.

We spent the rest of the evening talking about the movie and other things. As we left the mall, I could sense that Emily was feeling more comfortable around me. I was happy that I had been able to help her overcome her fear of horror movies. It was a great day spent having fun and spending time with Emily.

Emily's farewell was just two days away and she asked me what she should wear. I told her to wear whatever she liked because she always looked pretty in everything. She replied with a smile and said, "Okay!"

I couldn't wait for her farewell day, so I decided to surprise her by visiting her in college. As I walked past the outdoor area, I saw her with her classmates, clicking pictures. She looked absolutely gorgeous in a little reddish dress, wearing her tiny earrings and her hair flipped on one side. She looked too cute!

I couldn't help but stare at her beautiful smile as she laughed and joked with her friends. I felt a sudden urge to talk to her, but I didn't want to spoil her moment with her friends. I decided to wait until she was done taking pictures.

As soon as they finished taking pictures, she noticed me and came running towards me, giving me a tight hug. My heart was beating fast as it was the first time she had hugged me. She said, "Archer, what a surprise! You've made my day even more special. By the way, how do I look?"

At that moment, I didn't know what to say because she looked so beautiful. I finally replied, "You look so pretty and cute, just like always."

A few weeks had passed and things were going great between us. We had spent a lot of time together, watching movies, exploring the city, and trying out new restaurants. I felt that it was time for her to meet my parents, and I wanted to make sure that the introduction was comfortable and casual.

So, I suggested that we all go out for brunch together. I chose a laid-back restaurant that I knew my parents would enjoy, and made a reservation for the four of us. I was a little nervous on the day of the brunch, as I wanted everything to go smoothly and for my parents to like Emily as much as I did.

When we arrived at the restaurant, my parents were already there waiting for us. They greeted us warmly, and I introduced Emily to them. We all sat down at the table and ordered our food, making small talk as we waited for it to arrive.

As we ate, we talked about our interests and hobbies, and Emily shared stories about her family and childhood. My parents seemed to be enjoying themselves, and I could tell that they were impressed with Emily. She was charming, witty, and intelligent, and I could see that my parents were getting along with her quite well.

By the end of the meal, I felt relieved and happy that everything had gone so well. I dropped Emily off at her place and drove back home. A few hours later, my mom called me and said, "Emily is a sweet girl. Why don't you both date?"

I smiled and replied, "Mom, i want us to be bestfriends first." We both laughed and talked about how well the brunch had gone. I told her that I was planning to take things slow and get to know Emily better before jumping into a serious relationship.

My mom agreed and said, "That's a good idea. You don't want to rush into anything." I thanked her for her support

As I went to bed that night, I couldn't help but feel excited about the future. Emily was an amazing person, and I knew that we had a bright future ahead of us. I had a feeling that we were going to be together for a long time.

It was a typical day for me. I was sitting in my room, listening to some of my favorite tunes when suddenly, a message popped up on my computer screen. It immediately caught my attention. The message read, "Dear Mr. Archer D'Souza, your job approval has been accepted. We would like to inform you that you will need to join work by next week."

I was ecstatic to read this message. After months of job searching, I finally received the approval I was waiting for. I quickly read through the message again to make sure I wasn't dreaming.

As my excitement started to settle, I began to think about the new journey I was about to embark on. I was thrilled about the prospect of starting a new job, but I also felt a little nervous. The idea of starting a new job in a new place can be intimidating, but I was ready for the challenge.

I spent the rest of the night thinking about my upcoming job and what it would entail. I knew I had to start preparing myself for the next week, so I began to make a list of things I needed to do before starting my new job. I also started looking for a place to stay in the new city and researching about the place.

The more I thought about it, the more nervous I became. I had never lived outside of my hometown before and the thought of starting afresh in a new city was daunting. However, I was also excited about the opportunities that lay ahead of me. The job was in my dream field and I knew it was a great opportunity for me to learn and grow.

But there was one thing that was bothering me - I had to tell Emily about this and I had no idea how she would react. I knew that this news would be a shock for her. I decided to talk to her the next day and hoped for the best.

With all these thoughts in mind, I finally drifted off to sleep, dreaming about my new job and the life that awaited me in the new city.

I called Emily first thing in the morning and told her I had something important to share. She responded by saying that she, too, had something to tell me. We agreed to meet near the park at 5 PM and reveal our secrets to each other at the same time. Emily willingly agreed to the plan. Since it wasn't raining, I didn't bring an umbrella. However, Emily brought one just in case it rained. When we met, we counted to three and revealed our secrets simultaneously. Emily blushed and admitted that she was in love with me. But, my heart ached as I revealed that I had gotten a job offer in another state. We both knew that it was not the right time for us, and we stood there silently, listening to the sound of raindrops falling on the umbrella. The rain felt like a metaphor for the tears that we both wanted to shed. We hugged each other, knowing that it might be the last time we would see each other.

while"I couldn't hold it in any longer, so I finally mustered the courage to confess my love to her. I told her that I had loved her from the moment I met her, but unfortunately, our timing wasn't right today. She smiled sweetly and reassured me that my job was just as important as our love, and that we could still share our love over the phone. Her words filled my heart with warmth and comfort, and I knew in that moment that I had found my soulmate."

# IV

# Miles apart but close at heart

As I sat at the train station lost in my thoughts, I suddenly felt a tap on my shoulder. I turned around to see Emily running towards me with a big smile on her face.

"Thought you could leave without saying goodbye?" she said, breathless from running. I smiled and stood up to hug her. It was good to see her again. We had spent countless months being together, and she had been an important part of my life.

As we hugged, I could feel the warmth of her embrace and the familiar scent of her perfume. She pulled back and looked at me with a twinkle in her eye. "I'm going to miss you," she said.

"I'm going to miss you too," I replied, feeling a lump in my throat.

Emily gave me a kiss on the cheek, and we exchanged a few more words before I had to leave. As soon as my train arrived, I took my seat while she said, "Come back soon." I felt a lump in my throat as I watched her walk away, knowing that I would miss her terribly. The memories we had shared flooded my mind, and I couldn't help but feel emotional. As the train left the station, I wiped away a tear and promised myself that I would do everything in my power to see her again.

As I settled into my seat on the train, I knew it was going to be a long journey. I had a book to read, but I was also looking forward to watching the scenery pass by. As the night wore on, I found myself drifting off to sleep. When I woke up, I realized that the train had stopped at a station. I glanced out of the window, but I couldn't figure out where we were. The signs were all in a language I didn't understand.

Feeling a little groggy, I decided to get off the train and stretch my legs. As I stepped onto the platform, the cold air hit me, making me shiver. I looked around, taking in my surroundings. Despite the language barrier, I could tell that this was a small town. It seemed peaceful and quiet, with hardly anyone around.

After a few minutes of walking around, I felt refreshed and ready to continue my journey. I made my way back to the train and settled into my seat once again. As I reached for my bag, my stomach rumbled, reminding me that I hadn't eaten anything since the night before. I decided to head to the dining car to see what was on offer for breakfast.

As I walked through the train, I couldn't help but marvel at how different it was. The seats were more comfortable, the dining car was fancier, and the whole atmosphere was more relaxed. When I finally reached the dining car, I was greeted by the smell of fresh chai (tea). I ordered a plate of Samoosa and a cup of chai, and sat down to enjoy my breakfast.

As I sipped my chai, I couldn't help but feel grateful for this experience. Despite the language barrier and the unfamiliar surroundings, I was enjoying every moment of this journey.

After what felt like an eternity of waiting, the train finally started moving again. I let out a sigh of relief and settled back into my seat, grateful that I was one step closer to reaching my destination. With three more hours of the journey ahead, I decided to take the opportunity to enjoy the beautiful scenery outside.

As I gazed out of the window, I was struck by the sheer beauty of the landscape. The rolling hills, the vast expanse of greenery, and the winding rivers were a sight to behold.

I watched as the train chugged along the tracks, passing through quaint villages and bustling towns. The people going about their daily lives, the children playing in the fields, and the farmers tending to their crops all added to the enchanting scene outside.

As the journey continued, I found myself lost in thought, contemplating the beauty of nature and the fleeting nature of time. The passing scenery was a reminder that everything in life is temporary, and that we should take the time to appreciate the present moment.

With each passing mile, I felt a sense of peace and contentment wash over me. The journey was no longer just a means to an end, but a moment of reflection and introspection. And as the train slowly made its way towards my destination, I knew that I would carry this feeling of gratitude and appreciation with me for a long time to come.

After a long journey, the train finally reached my destination - the bustling city of Chennai. Formerly known as Madras, Chennai is the capital city of Tamil Nadu, the southernmost state of India. The city is also the state's primate city and is located on the Coromandel Coast of the Bay of Bengal. Chennai is one of the most popular tourist destinations in India, known for its rich culture, history, architecture, and food.

As I stepped out of the train, I was greeted by the warm and humid air of Chennai. The city is known for its tropical climate, with hot temperatures and heavy rainfall throughout the year. Despite the weather, Chennai is a vibrant and lively city that never sleeps. The streets are always bustling with people, cars, and motorcycles, creating a chaotic yet charming atmosphere.

As I made my way through the busy streets, I couldn't help but notice the beautiful architecture of the buildings around me. Chennai is home to some of the most stunning examples of Dravidian architecture, a style that originated in South India over 2,000 years ago. The city is also known for its colonial-era buildings, which stand in stark contrast to the traditional Indian architecture.

I had an important interview to attend, so I decided to book a motel for a day or two. It was close to the venue, and I wanted to ensure that I was well-rested and prepared for the interview. I was nervous and anxious as this was a job that I've always dreamed of and I didn't want to mess it up.

As soon as I reached the motel, I remembered that I hadn't spoken to Emily since last night. She was my girlfriend, and she always supported me in everything I did. I immediately called her to let her know that I had reached safely. When I told her about the interview, she was incredibly supportive and encouraging. She said, "Don't worry, I know you will do it." Her words meant a lot to me, and they helped to calm my nerves. It was reassuring to know that I had someone who believed in me and my abilities.

After we hung up, I spent some time going over my notes and preparing for the interview. I wanted to make sure that I was well-prepared and confident when the time came. I went over the job requirements, the company's mission, and everything that I could think of to make sure that I had all the information I needed.

The next day, I went to the interview, feeling ready and focused. I did my best and gave it my all, knowing that I had the support of my lover behind me. The interview went well, and I felt like I had answered all the questions to the best of my ability.

After the interview, I got a call from the company, and they told me that I had been selected for the job. I was thrilled beyond words, and I couldn't wait to tell Emily about it. When I called her, she was over the moon with joy, and she congratulated me on my achievement. She said that she always knew that I could do it, and she was proud of me.

To make things even better, the company offered me a place to stay and transport to travel. It was an incredible opportunity, and I couldn't be happier. I knew that this was all possible because of the support and encouragement that I received from Emily. She was truly a great support system, and I knew that I could always count on her to be there for me when I needed her.

Every day at work felt like an endless battle, with my to-do list getting longer and longer. Juggling multiple projects at once, I found myself struggling to find any time for myself, let alone for my dear Emily. It had been days since we last spoke properly, and I missed her terribly.

I knew I needed to find a way to balance my work and personal life, but it felt impossible. No matter how much I tried, there was always more work to be done with endless emails to answer, calls to make, and deadlines to meet. I felt like I was being overwhelmed by my workload and couldn't see a way out.

At the same time, I was deeply concerned about Emily, who had been going through a hard time lately. She had lost her job and was struggling to find a new one. She was feeling down and anxious, and I knew that she needed my support more than ever. However, with my busy schedule, it felt like I was unable to be there for her.

I tried to make time for her, but it seemed like every time I started to work on a project, the phone would ring or an email would come in, taking up more of my time. I felt like I was being pulled in a hundred different directions, and I couldn't keep up.

As the days went by, I began to feel more and more helpless. I longed for a break, a moment of peace and quiet, or a chance to catch my breath and think. Sadly, it seemed like that was too much to ask for.

After months of working tirelessly, I finally got a chance to make a few friends at work. We were all busy with our respective tasks, but as our schedules became less hectic, we decided to go out for dinner. It was a much-needed break from our daily routine and a great opportunity to get to know each other better.

We chose a cozy little restaurant with a warm atmosphere and delicious food. As we sat down, we started talking about our work, our hobbies, and our interests. It was amazing to see how much we had in common, despite coming from different backgrounds and having different personalities. We laughed, shared stories, and even made plans for a weekend trip.

The food was excellent, and the service was impeccable. We enjoyed every moment of our time together, and before we knew it, it was time to head back home. As we said our goodbyes, we decided to go out at least once a week.

That dinner night was not just about food and drinks, it was about building relationships and creating memories. It reminded me that work is not just about meeting deadlines and hitting targets, it's also about connecting with people, making friends, and having fun.

❧

It's been a whole year since I moved to Chennai. Time has flown by so quickly! i have had the opportunity to speak with Emily on a few occasions.and I have enjoyed every conversation with her. However, I cannot help but worry that she might think something else about me because I have been so busy with my work lately.

I do not want Emily to feel like I am ignoring her or not interested in our relationship. I value her as a partner, and I would hate for something as trivial as my busy work schedule to come in the way of our bond. I know that she understands the nature of my work, but I still cannot shake off this feeling of guilt.

Nevertheless, I am determined to make more time for Emily. I believe that a true relationship requires effort and commitment from both parties, and I am willing to put in the work. I hope that Emily will see that my intentions are pure and that I genuinely care about our relationship.

❧

Finally, days later when they told me at work that I was going to be transferred back to my state. I couldn't wait to surprise Emily.

# V
## Only You!

"When I told my parents that I was returning home for good, my heart was already filled with anticipation for what was to come. After a long year of living away, what I needed most was to be back in my hometown, surrounded by the people I loved most, and most importantly, with my soulmate. I wanted to surprise my dearest Emily, whom I had missed with every fiber of my being. We planned a romantic dinner at my place, and I spent hours preparing her favorite dish as she sat at the dining table, I closed her eyes with my hands, her touch sent shivers down my spine, and I could feel my heart racing with excitement. She immediately realized it was me and screamed with joy, and as I gazed into her eyes, I could see the love and happiness shining through.

It was an emotional moment for both of us. We had shared countless memories, both happy and sad, and had always been there for each other. As Emily hugged me, tears welled up in her eyes, and she whispered, 'I missed you so much.'

In that moment, I knew that coming back home was the right decision. Being back with the people I loved most, surrounded by their warmth and support, filled my heart with joy and contentment. And as I sat there, surrounded by the people who meant the world to me, and most importantly, with my beloved Emily by my side, I knew that I was truly home, and that nothing could ever keep us apart."

After joining my new job, I found myself with a lot less work than before. This allowed me to finally give Emily the attention and time she deserved. I had been looking forward to this for a while, and it felt great to finally be able to focus on our relationship without any work-related distractions.

Despite Emily's unpredictable shift work, we made sure to keep in touch and meet up regularly. Our schedules sometimes conflicted, with Emily working morning-to-afternoon or afternoon-to-night shifts. But no matter what, we always found a way to make time for each other.

We would often go on dates, trying out new restaurants and exploring different parts of the city. On other nights, we would stay in and watch romantic movies together, cuddled up on the couch with some popcorn and a bottle of wine. It was these little moments that made our relationship special, and I was grateful for every one of them.

One sunny afternoon, Emily invited me over to her place for lunch. We had been dating for a while, and I was excited to finally meet her parents. As I walked into their neat and cozy house, I was greeted with warm hugs from Emily's parents. Emily's mother, a plump and friendly woman, asked me how everyone at home was doing. I replied, "We are all doing great, thanks for asking."

However, as soon as Emily's father, a tall and stern-looking man, caught sight of me, he gave me a rather intimidating stare. His eyes seemed to pierce through my soul, and I could feel my palms getting sweaty. He asked me what I did for a living, and I told him that I was an assistant manager at a well-known company.

Emily noticed the tension and quickly intervened, "Enough with all this talk, let's have lunch together, Dad." We all sat down at the table, and Emily's mother started serving the food. We had a hearty meal, and I must say, Emily's mother was an excellent cook.

During lunch, we talked about various things, including my hobbies, interests, and work life. I got to know Emily's parents better, and they seemed to warm up to me slowly. Emily's father even shared some stories from his younger days, and I could see that he was not as stern as I had first thought him to be.

After lunch, we all sat down in the living room and watched a movie together. It was a comedy, and we all laughed heartily at the jokes. It was a great way to unwind after a delicious meal.

As I was leaving, Emily's father shook my hand and said, "It was nice meeting you." I felt relieved that things had gone well, and Emily and I hugged each other tightly before I left. Overall, it was a pleasant afternoon, and I was happy to have spent it with Emily's family.

On my way back home, I couldn't help but feel grateful for Emily and her family's hospitality. They had made me feel welcome and comfortable despite my nervousness. I knew that I had made a good impression on them, and I looked forward to spending more time with them in the future.

As the winter season approached, the charm of weddings started to spread around. Emily, my girlfriend, invited me to her cousin Sheryl's wedding. I was ecstatic to attend the wedding with her. I got dressed up and picked up Emily and her parents. Being a gentleman, I escorted them to the wedding location. The ambiance was breathtakingly beautiful, with colorful lights, flowers and soothing music playing in the background.

We picked a table to sit down and enjoy the wedding ceremony. As we were conversing, Emily's cousins showed up and started asking her when we were getting married. Emily blushed and replied that she didn't know. I was surprised to find out that most of her cousins already knew me. I asked Emily how they knew I was her boyfriend, and she replied that she wanted everyone to know me and like me.

It was a pleasant surprise for me, and it made me feel happy to know that she was proud of me. As the wedding ceremony progressed, we enjoyed the food, music and the company of our friends. It was a memorable evening, and we danced the night away.

As the night was coming to an end, we walked out of the wedding venue, hand in hand, enjoying the chilly winter breeze. We talked about our future plans and our dreams for the future. It was a beautiful moment, and I felt grateful to have her in my life.

The bride and groom looked stunning, and their love for each other was evident in their eyes. The wedding ceremony was a reminder of the love and commitment that two individuals share, and it made us realize the importance of cherishing every moment that we spend with each other. The winter season may be cold and harsh, but it also brings with it the warmth of love and togetherness, which we should hold dear in our hearts.

# VI

## Love you a little more...

For days, I had been consumed by the thought of how to set up the perfect marriage proposal for Emily. We had been together for what felt like an eternity, and I knew in my heart that she was the one I wanted to spend the rest of my life with. But I also knew that I had to make this proposal special, something that she would never forget.

I spent hours researching different ideas and scenarios, trying to come up with the perfect plan. I wanted it to be romantic, but not cliche; personal, but not too over the top. It was a delicate balance, and I knew that I had to get it just right.

As the days went on, my anxiety grew. I could feel the weight of the proposal bearing down on me, and I knew that I couldn't wait much longer. Finally, I decided on a plan, and I set everything in motion.

The night of the proposal was a blur of nerves and excitement. I had never been so nervous in my life, but I knew that I had to push through it. I had arranged a private dinner at a rooftop restaurant overlooking the city, where we had enjoyed some of our most memorable moments together.

As we sat there, savoring the delicious food and talking about our future plans, I felt my heart racing. I knew that the moment was approaching, and I could barely contain my excitement. Suddenly, the lights went out, and the entire city skyline lit up with fireworks.

I turned to Emily, who was gazing up at the sky in wonder, and took her hand. As she turned to me, I got down on one knee and asked her to be my wife. Tears streamed down her face as she said yes, and I knew in that moment that I had made the right decision.

The rest of the night was a blur of champagne toasts, excited phone calls to friends and family, and endless laughter. It was a moment that I will never forget and one that I know we will cherish for the rest of our lives. And now, as we plan our future together, I am filled with excitement and gratitude for the love that we share.

It was a beautiful evening, and Emily's place was filled with the aroma of delicious food. Everyone was sitting around the table, enjoying the meal, and having a conversation. We were discussing our decision to get married, and both of our families were excited about it. It was a moment of joy, and we were all happy to be together.

During the conversation, Emily's father hugged me and said, "Love my daughter a lot and never make her cry." Those words touched my heart, and I could feel the sincerity in his voice. I replied, "I will always love her more than anything in life." I meant every word, and I knew that my love for her would never fade away.

I was surprised when Emily's father hugged me as when we had first met, I thought he didn't like me. Now I know that all men often hide their feelings towards the person they love. They act as if they don't care, but deep down, they do care about you a lot. It was a moment of realization for me, and I felt grateful for having such a wonderful father-in-law.

As the night went on, we continued to talk about our future plans. We discussed how we would build a family, and how we would take care of each other. It was a beautiful moment, and we all felt blessed to be together.

In the end, we all agreed that love is the most important thing in life. It brings people together and makes life worth living. Emily's father hugged me again, and this time I felt like I was part of the family. I knew that I had found the love of my life, and I was ready to embark on a new journey with her.

We had been planning our engagement for quite some time now. We wanted to keep it simple yet memorable, something that would reflect our personalities and our love for each other. After a lot of discussions and brainstorming, we finally decided to host the ceremony at Emily's place. We both wanted to keep the guest list limited to our close family and friends, as we wanted to make the event intimate and personal.

As we started planning, we realized that it was going to be a bit of a challenge to manage everything on our own. That's when our cousins stepped in to help us. They offered to assist us with the outdoor decor and also serve snacks and drinks to our guests. We were grateful for their help, and it was such a relief to have them take care of these things. They added a personal touch to the ceremony and made sure that everything was perfect.

On the other hand, our friends came up with the idea of arranging transportation for our guests. They also volunteered to help us with any other things that we might need. We were so touched by their kindness and willingness to help us. It made us realize how lucky we were to have such amazing friends who were always there for us, no matter what.

Our close friend, Sybil, had been living abroad for quite some time. She had come back to Goa just in time for our engagement ceremony. As soon as she entered Emily's house, she hugged us both and congratulated us on our engagement. With excitement in her voice, she told Emily that she had always believed that we were perfect for each other and that I would keep her happy always. Emily, blushing, replied with agreement that indeed she was right. As the party started, we all enjoyed the night dancing and having fun to the beat of the music.

We were so happy to have all of our loved ones with us on our special day. It was a beautiful evening filled with love, laughter, and happiness. We were both grateful for the love and support that we had received from our family and friends. It was a day that we would always cherish and remember, a day that marked the beginning of our journey together as partners in life. We were excited for what the future held and looked forward to sharing more memorable moments with our loved ones.

One summer evening, Emily and I were returning home from a concert. We had been so excited for this concert for weeks, and we had an absolute blast singing and dancing along to our favorite band. However, on the drive back, something unexpected happened.

Suddenly, Emily felt something happening to her, and she blurted out, "Stop the car!" I could sense the panic in her voice and immediately pulled the car over to the side of the road. I asked her what had happened, and she said she felt weak and was struggling to breathe.

At first, I thought it might be because we had just returned from a crowded concert. So, I rolled down the windows to let some fresh air in, but it didn't seem to help. I told her to drink water, and she took a sip, but then suddenly collapsed. I was terrified about what had happened and tried sprinkling water on her face to wake her up, but that didn't work either.

I realized that we needed to get her medical attention quickly, so I started the car and raced her to the nearest hospital. It was a long and anxious drive, and I kept praying that she would be okay. Finally, we reached the hospital, and I immediately rushed her into the emergency room.

The medical staff quickly attended to her and ran some tests. as the doctor told me it will take a day to get the report I informed both of our parents about what had happened to Emily, and they arrived quickly. We all waited outside while Emily's mom was with her in the room.

The night was long, and we had barely slept. The reason was our concern for Emily. And we knew she was going through a tough time. We all sat there, waiting for the reports to come, hoping for the best but fearing the worst.

As the morning light started to peek through the window, we could feel the anxiety building up. Finally, the doctor arrived with the reports, and we all gathered around him, eagerly waiting for the news.

Our worst fears came true when the doctor informed us that Emily had entered stage 2 cancer. We were all shocked to hear this news. The room fell silent, and we could hear nothing but our own thoughts.

On the other side, Emily's parents were inconsolable. They couldn't believe that their daughter, who was so full of life, was fighting such a terrible disease. I tried to console them by saying that Emily is a strong girl and will fight this battle bravely.

We spent the rest of the day at the hospital, talking to Emily and trying to lift her spirits. She was scared, but her willpower was unbreakable. She was determined to fight this disease and come out victorious.

In the coming weeks, we stood by Emily, offering all the support we could. We helped her with her appointments, cooked her meals, and spent time with her. We watched as she went through chemotherapy and radiation therapy, and we were amazed by her strength and courage.

Finally, after months of fighting, Emily was declared cancer-free. We were overjoyed to hear this news, and we knew that Emily's strength and willpower had played a significant role in her recovery.

This experience taught us all a valuable lesson about life, love, and the importance of being there for each other. We realized that even in the darkest of times, there is always hope, and with the support of our loved ones, we can overcome any obstacle that comes our way.

❧

❧

But Was this really The End of the Beginning ? or The Beginning of an End?

❧

❧

## A YEAR LATER...

We had been waiting for this day for so long, and it finally came. We knew that we had to celebrate this milestone in a big way, and what better way to do that than getting married? We started planning our wedding with great enthusiasm, and it quickly became our favorite topic of conversation.

We spent hours browsing through wedding magazines and websites, looking for inspiration and ideas. We discussed every detail, from the color scheme and the flowers to the menu and the music. We wanted everything to be perfect, a reflection of our love and commitment to each other.

As we worked on the preparations, we also reflected on the journey that brought us here. We remembered the sleepless nights in the hospital, the endless rounds of chemotherapy and radiation, and the uncertainty and fear that we had to face. But we also remembered the moments of hope and resilience, the small victories that kept us going, and the love and support of our family and friends.

Now, as we looked forward to our wedding day, we felt grateful for each other and for the life that we had. We knew that the road ahead would not be easy, but we were ready to face it together, with the same strength and courage that brought us here. We knew that our love was stronger than any adversity, and that we could overcome anything as long as we had each other.

We were excited to start this new chapter in our lives, as husband and wife, and we knew that our journey together would be filled with love, joy, and endless possibilities. We were grateful for this second chance at life, and we were determined to make the most of it.

Today was a significant day for us as we were finally getting married. I can hardly believe that this day has finally arrived after months of planning and anticipation. I started my day by waking up early and preparing for the day's activities with my best men, while Emily and her bridesmaids were already getting ready at her place.

As I got dressed, I couldn't help but feel a mix of excitement and nervousness. I knew that this was going to be one of the most important days of my life, and I wanted everything to go perfectly.

Once I was dressed and ready, I headed over to the venue where the ceremony was going to take place. As I arrived, I was greeted by our friends and family who had come from far and wide to celebrate this special day with us.

The venue was decorated beautifully with flowers and candles, and I couldn't help but feel a sense of awe as I looked around. I knew that Emily had put so much time and effort into making everything perfect, and it truly showed.

As I stood at the altar, waiting for my bride-to-be to make her grand entrance, I felt a mix of emotions - excitement, nervousness, and overwhelming joy. I couldn't wait to see Emily walking down the aisle towards me, and when she finally arrived, she looked absolutely stunning. The way her white dress flowed behind her and the smile on her face made me feel like the luckiest man in the world.

The ceremony was beautiful, filled with heartfelt vows and beautiful music. I remember feeling a sense of calm wash over me as we exchanged rings and were pronounced husband and wife. It was a moment that I will cherish forever.

After the ceremony, we celebrated with a reception that was filled with laughter, dancing, and of course, delicious food. Our guests had a great time, and we were so happy to see everyone enjoying themselves. We danced the night away, taking in every moment of the celebration.

Looking back on that day, I'filled with gratitude for the people who made it all possible - our families, friends, and everyone who helped to bring our vision to life. It was a day that we will never forget, and I am so grateful to have shared it with the people who mean the most to us.

As time progressed, it felt like everything was transpiring in a blur. Before we knew it, half a year had elapsed since our wedding day. Although it had only been six months, we had already undergone our fair share of quarrels and disagreements. Some were over the TV remote, while others were over trivial things like me leaving my damp towel on the bed after bathing. But even when Emily's face was contorted in anger, I couldn't help but find it endearing.

Despite the occasional disputes, we were content. We had constructed a life together and were discovering how to navigate through the ebbs and flows that accompanied marriage. We cooked together, embarked on adventures, and created memories.

On a beautiful day, the sun was shining bright and the birds were chirping, as we took a leisurely stroll down the street. We were surrounded by the sights and sounds of the bustling city, filled with people going about their day. As we walked, we came across a vibrant play school, filled with tiny tots laughing and playing with their toys. The innocence and joy on their faces struck a chord within us, filling our hearts with an inexplicable happiness.

The energy and excitement of the little ones was infectious, and we found ourselves drawn to the school. We stood there for a few moments, watching them play and interact with each other. It was as if their laughter had cast a spell on us, and we could feel an overwhelming urge to be parents. The thought of holding our own child and experiencing the joys of parenthood was simply irresistible.

Emily and I shared a warm smile, knowing that we both shared this desire. We had talked about starting a family for a while, but something about seeing those little kids filled us with a renewed sense of purpose. We knew that we were ready to take on the challenge of parenthood and all that it entailed.

As we continued our walk, the memory of those little kids and their carefree laughter lingered in our minds, reminding us that someday, we too would be blessed with our own little bundle of joy. We knew that it wouldn't be easy, but we were ready to take the leap and start our family. And as we walked hand in hand, we couldn't help but feel excited for the future and all the wonderful things that it held.

# VII

## Love Her a little more...

Two weeks had passed, and the news of my partner's pregnancy had filled our lives with joy and excitement. It was a moment we had been eagerly waiting for, and it had finally come. From the moment we found out, we knew that our lives were about to change forever. We were thrilled but nervous at the same time, wondering how we would handle the responsibilities that come with parenthood.

I knew that with the changes her body was undergoing, I had to take extra care of her. I made sure that she was eating healthy, taking her vitamins, and getting enough rest. I would carry her bags, open doors for her, and even massage her feet when they got sore. I wanted to make sure that she felt loved and supported every step of the way.

Together, we spent countless hours discussing baby names, nursery themes, and parenting styles. We read books, watched videos, and talked to other parents to prepare ourselves as much as possible. We wanted to make sure that we were doing everything we could to bring our baby into a safe and comfortable environment.

As the days went by, Emily's baby bump grew bigger and bigger, and we eagerly awaited the arrival of our little one. We would spend hours talking to the baby, feeling its kicks and movements, and imagining what it would be like to hold it in our arms. We were filled with a sense of wonder and amazement at the miracle of life growing inside her.

Despite the moments of uncertainty and worry, we knew that we were in this together and that we would be good parents. We knew that there would be challenges ahead, but we were ready to face them head-on. We were determined to give our child the best life possible, filled with love, support, and opportunities for growth.

As the days turned into weeks, and weeks into months, I continued to take care of Emily throughout her pregnancy. It was a time of great anticipation, as we eagerly awaited the arrival of our little one. Emily's body was undergoing tremendous changes, and I was amazed at her strength and resilience throughout it all. I knew that it was my duty to ensure her safety and the safety of our unborn child, and I took that responsibility very seriously.

I made it a point to be there for Emily every single day, doing everything I could to make her life easier and more comfortable. I would wake up early to cook her favorite breakfasts, and I would spend my evenings running errands and doing chores around the house so that she could rest and relax. I never allowed her to lift anything heavy or do any strenuous work, as I knew that she needed to take it easy and avoid any unnecessary stress.

As the due date approached, I could feel the excitement building within me. I couldn't wait to hold our little one in my arms and to see Emily's face light up with joy. Despite the challenges and uncertainties that came with pregnancy, I felt incredibly lucky to be able to support Emily during such an important and transformative time in her life.

The delivery room was a flurry of activity as Emily and I prepared for the arrival of our baby. Outside, the expectant grandparents waited nervously, eager for news of the little one's arrival.

Amid the chaos, we found a moment of calm. I reached out to take Emilys hand, offering a steady presence in the face of the pain and uncertainty that lay ahead. As the doctor gave instructions and the countdown began, we locked eyes, drawing strength from one another.

In that moment, we were two individuals united in a singular purpose. we had come this far together, and we were determined to see it through to the end. With a deep breath and a silent prayer, we braced ourselves for what was to come.

For Emily, the pain was intense, a fierce wave that threatened to overwhelm her. But i was there, every step of the way, offering words of encouragement and a strong shoulder to lean on. Together, we pushed through the agony, counting to three and giving it everything we had.

And then, in the blink of an eye, it was over. The baby had arrived, a tiny bundle of joy that would change our lives forever. As soon as the words "it's a girl" left the doctor's mouth, our faces were instantly lit up with joy and excitement. It was a beautiful Saturday evening when our daughter finally made her grand entrance at precisely 10:30 PM. The room was filled with excitement and joy as we held our little one for the very first time. After much discussion, Emily and I had decided on the perfect name for our daughter: Lilly. The name Lilly had always been a favorite of ours, and we knew it was the perfect fit for our precious little girl. As we looked down at her tiny fingers and toes, we couldn't help but feel overwhelmed with emotion. We knew that from that moment on, our lives would forever be changed. As we cradled our newborn in our arms, surrounded by proud grandparents and the glow of new parenthood, we knew that this was just the beginning of an incredible journey.

As the phone rang incessantly, with each incoming call came a wave of joy and excitement that seemed to fill the room with a palpable energy. Our hearts were bursting with happiness as we held our newborn baby girl in our arms, marveling at the miracle of life. The sound of familiar voices congratulating us on her arrival echoed through the halls, making us feel like we were surrounded by a loving and supportive community.

The moment was unforgettable, one that marked the beginning of a new chapter in our lives. We knew that from that day on, nothing would ever be the same. We were filled with a sense of wonder and awe, amazed at the tiny, perfect human being we had brought into the world. And as we looked around at the smiling faces of our friends and family, we felt an overwhelming sense of gratitude for the love and support that surrounded us.

In that moment, anything felt possible. We knew that the road ahead would be full of challenges, but we also knew that we had each other, and that we were surrounded by a community of people who loved us and believed in us. It was a moment of pure joy and possibility, one that we would hold in our hearts forever.

The day Emily was discharged from the hospital and we welcomed our newborn baby, Lily, into our home, was one of the most joyous moments of our lives. We had been eagerly waiting for this day, making elaborate preparations to create a warm and welcoming environment for our little one.

As we entered our house with Lily in our arms, our cousins and family members rushed to greet us, their faces beaming with excitement and anticipation. It was a moment of pure delight and happiness, watching everyone come together to shower our little one with love and affection.

The atmosphere was electric, filled with laughter, tears of joy, and an overwhelming sense of gratitude. Holding Lily in our arms, we felt blessed to have her in our lives, and we knew that this moment would be etched in our memories forever.

As the days wore on, our nights grew restless and fraught with anxiety as we tended to Lily, whose inconsolable cries echoed through the house. We tried everything within our means to soothe her, but every attempt proved futile, leaving us exhausted in body and spirit.

Yet, we refused to be defeated by this challenge. We toiled tirelessly, determined to find the solution that would bring our little one the peace she deserved. We delved into countless books and articles, experimented with every remedy we could find, and persisted through the darkest of nights.

Finally, after what felt like an eternity of searching, we stumbled upon a revelation. By playing gentle melodies and massaging her tenderly, we were able to ease her into a tranquil slumber, and with it, came a newfound sense of relief and joy.

The night had slowly crept up on us, enveloping us in its inky embrace. Lily had drifted off to sleep, her chest rising and falling in a peaceful rhythm. Emily and I remained, basking in the quietude of the moment. Suddenly, Emily's playful voice interrupted the peaceful silence, "Now, whom do you love more, me or Lily?"

I was caught off guard by her question but knew that honesty was the only way forward. I replied, "I love her a little more than you." Emily's face lit up with a playful smile as she held me, resting her head on my shoulder.

As we sat there, I couldn't help but marvel at how fortunate I was to have these two remarkable women in my life. Lily, with her infectious laughter and playful antics, brought a sense of innocence and wonder to my life, while Emily, with her warm embrace and gentle nature, brought me a sense of calm and comfort. It was in moments like these that I knew that I was loved beyond measure and that my life was full of blessings that I could never have imagined.

As I gazed upon the crowd, enraptured by the joyous celebration of life, I couldn't help but feel a sense of wonder at the passage of time. It was hard to believe that a year had already passed since the birth of Lily, this precious bundle of life and love.

The room was filled with the sounds of laughter and the sweet melodies of music, as we all gathered to mark this momentous occasion. And yet, amidst the revelry and merriment, there was a sense of reflection and introspection that hung in the air.

For in the brief span of a year, we had watched Lily grow and evolve into a captivating little girl, full of wonder and curiosity. We had shared in her first steps, her first words, and the boundless energy and enthusiasm that she brought into our lives.

As I looked around the room, I couldn't help but feel a deep sense of gratitude for the love and joy that Lily had brought into our lives. And as we sang "Happy Birthday" and blew out the candles on her birthday cake, I knew that this was just the beginning of a lifelong journey filled with adventure, curiosity, and boundless possibility.

The sun had set on a quiet evening when Lily's birthday celebrations came to a close. It was then that Emily began to experience aches and pains in various parts of her body, the likes of which she had never felt before. At first, we attributed it to the stress of dealing with a one-year-old who was constantly awake and in need of attention.

However, as the days went by, the pains only seemed to get worse. With each passing moment, Emily's anxiety grew. We decided to seek medical attention, and after several tests and examinations, we were told that we would receive the results later that evening.

As we waited in the doctor's office,our hearts pounding with apprehension, we tried to remain hopeful. But when the doctor returned with the test results, our world was shattered.

Emily's cancer had returned, and this time, it was far more relentless. It had spread to other parts of her body, and the prognosis was grim. The doctors didn't sugarcoat it—she had reached the final stage of cancer, also known as advanced cancer. It was a reality that hit us like a tidal wave. The weight of the news crushed us, but somehow, we tried to remain hopeful, holding on to the idea that there was still a chance, a sliver of hope. Yet, even with a 50% survival rate, we knew deep in our hearts that the road ahead would be anything but easy.

The hospital room was silent except for the soft beeping of machines and the rustle of the sterile white sheets. Emily lay there, her frail body hooked up to tubes and wires. Her eyes, wide with fear, betrayed the strength she tried so hard to maintain. She looked so alone in that hospital bed, and my heart broke seeing her like this. I rushed to her side, taking her trembling hand in mine. Her warmth gave me some comfort, though it was tinged with the reality of her fragile state. I had to be strong—for her, for us, for everything we still had left.

Leaning in close, I whispered the words I knew she needed to hear, "Everything will be alright, Emily. You will be alright. Nothing will happen to you. I'm here with you, and we will fight this together."

Her eyes met mine, a flicker of relief passing through them. She nodded, though it was clear she didn't believe the words completely. But I had to believe them for both of us. I had to believe that together, we could face whatever came next.

As the days passed, our lives became a blur of hospital visits, doctors' appointments, and the relentless cycle of treatments. We tried to maintain a semblance of normalcy, but Emily's condition worsened. The cancer had spread too far, and the chemotherapy, while necessary, left her weak and bedridden.

It was then that we made the decision to bring her home.

There was a certain heaviness in our hearts as we packed up her things at the hospital, knowing that the journey home would mark a new chapter, one filled with bittersweet moments. Emily had always been the heart of our family, the one who brought warmth and joy into our lives. Now, we had to find a way to bring that same sense of home and comfort back to her, even as she lay bedridden, unable to move or enjoy the simple pleasures of life she once loved.

We spent hours planning her room, making sure it was as comforting and familiar as possible. We covered the bed with her favorite soft blankets and pillows, the ones she used to curl up with on lazy Sundays. Pictures of loved ones were hung on the walls, each frame a reminder of the beautiful moments we had shared. We even installed a TV so that Emily could watch her favorite shows and movies, hoping that it would offer her some distraction from the pain.

Our daughter, Lily, was too young to fully understand the depth of the situation, but she knew something was wrong. She would sit by Emily's side, her small hand resting gently on her mother's arm, asking questions that were hard to answer. "Mommy, when will you be better?" Lily would ask, her eyes wide with innocence and worry. It was a question I didn't know how to answer.

But despite the sadness that seemed to hang in the air like a storm cloud, Lily was also a source of light. Her laughter, her boundless energy, and her love for her mother were the things that gave us moments of respite, even in the darkest times. Emily would smile softly at Lily, her eyes filled with a tenderness that only a mother's heart could hold. Lily had the ability to bring a sense of normalcy to a world that had been turned upside down.

We took turns caring for Emily, making sure she was comfortable, attending to her needs, and just being there. We spent hours by her bedside, talking, reminiscing about the past, sharing stories of Lily's latest adventures, and just being together. It was hard not to feel overwhelmed, but in those moments, we held on to each other.

Though it was impossible to ignore the grim reality of Emily's condition, we made an effort to treasure the time we had. We couldn't predict the future, but we knew that the present was all we could control. So, we focused on making the most of every moment.

We laughed, we cried, we remembered, and we hoped. We knew the road ahead would be difficult, but as long as we had each other, we would face it together.

Emily's smile, weak though it was, was all the proof we needed to know that we were doing the right thing. Even in the face of such pain and uncertainty, there was love. And in that love, we found the strength to continue.

No matter what came next, we would fight together. And through it all, Lily's innocence and love reminded us that there were still beautiful moments to be found, even in the hardest of times.

The days began to blur together, one after another, each carrying its own set of challenges. Emily's strength seemed to ebb and flow with the hours, her body weak from the treatments and the relentless spread of the cancer. Some days, she would wake up, her eyes flickering with a spark of her old self—playful, determined, even if just for a moment. Other days, the pain would leave her distant, her eyes glassy, as though she was retreating to some place far from us.

But Lily... Lily kept us grounded. She had this incredible ability to light up the room, even on the darkest days. Each morning, she would rush into Emily's room, a colorful drawing in hand—her latest masterpiece for her mommy. "Look, Mommy!" she'd exclaim, holding up the picture with excitement. "It's us, all together! See? I drew the sun because we're all going to be okay!"

Sometimes Emily would smile, a weak but genuine smile that filled the room with warmth. Other times, her eyes would glisten with unshed tears, but she would blink them away before anyone could notice. Lily didn't fully understand why Mommy couldn't get out of bed or why Daddy's eyes were often red-rimmed, but she knew enough to know that her love was the greatest gift she could offer.

Her little arms wrapped around Emily's fragile body in tight hugs that made both of them feel better, if only for a moment.

The house, once bustling with the sounds of daily life, had become quieter. The hum of the refrigerator and the occasional clink of dishes in the kitchen were the only sounds that filled the air when Lily wasn't running through the house, playing with her dolls or making up stories. We had a routine, of sorts—dinner at the table, with Emily sitting in her chair, though she didn't eat much anymore. The room would fall silent as we tried to carry on, as though the world outside could still be normal, even if our world inside was changing drastically.

But those moments of normalcy, however fleeting, were our lifeline.

I began to notice something in Emily's eyes. It wasn't fear anymore. No, it was something more profound—a kind of acceptance. She knew the gravity of the situation, yet she still fought. For herself. For Lily. For me. I think, in a way, Emily had found some peace in her acceptance, though it came with its own heartache. There were nights when we would lie together, her head resting on my chest, and I would whisper about all the beautiful things we had lived through together—the trips we took, the holidays we celebrated, the laughter we shared. I would tell her how strong she was, how brave. How much she meant to me, to Lily, to everyone who had been touched by her warmth.

"I don't know how much time we have," Emily whispered one night, her voice barely audible. "But I want you and Lily to keep going, no matter what happens. I want you to promise me that."

I squeezed her hand tighter, brushing a lock of her hair from her forehead. "I promise, Emily. I promise we will."

And I meant it. With all my heart.

As the weeks passed, Emily's condition continued to deteriorate. She spent more time asleep than awake, her body weak and frail. But even in those quiet moments, we tried to surround her with love. We would play her favorite songs softly in the background, songs that had been the soundtrack of our life together. Sometimes we would watch old movies, the kind that made us laugh, remembering how we'd watched them as a couple before Lily was born.

The house became a sanctuary, a place where we could hold on to what little was left. Every afternoon, I would take Lily into the garden, where she would pick flowers and tell me stories about imaginary worlds. "Mommy's going to get better," she would say, her eyes wide with a mix of hope and innocence. I would nod, holding her hand tightly, though a knot formed in my chest. Lily couldn't understand the finality of it all, but that didn't make her words any less meaningful.

In those moments, I clung to the hope that Emily had given me—that somehow, we could find strength in the love we had, no matter how much time we had left. I had to believe it, for Emily, for Lily, and for me.

But as much as we tried to live in the present, the future loomed large, always in the back of my mind. There were nights when I would sit next to Emily, watching her breathe, trying to memorize every detail of her face, every soft breath she took. The thought that I might have to say goodbye one day soon was a thought I couldn't even begin to process. But in those moments, I did my best to push it away, focusing only on the now.

One evening, as the sun set and the sky outside turned shades of orange and pink, Emily opened her eyes, just enough to meet mine. Her gaze was tired, but there was something in it—something that made me lean in closer.

"I love you," she whispered, her voice rough but filled with meaning. "And I love Lily."

Tears welled up in my eyes, but I forced them back. "I love you too, Emily. So much."

She smiled, a faint but beautiful smile that was all her own. "Take care of her. Take care of Lily. She's going to need you."

And I knew then, with all my heart, that no matter what happened, I would keep that promise. I would protect her, protect Lily, and I would carry Emily's love with me, always.

The following days were quiet, a mix of waiting, of being together, and of cherishing each precious moment. We all held on to the love that had been the foundation of our family, the thing that had always seen us through even the toughest of times.

And through it all, Lily, with her innocent heart and unwavering love, continued to remind us that, even in the face of darkness, there was still light.

The weeks continued to pass, and though Emily's condition fluctuated, there was something undeniable in the way she was holding on—fighting harder than any of us expected. We had prepared ourselves for the worst, for the inevitable, but somehow, Emily kept pushing through. The treatments were exhausting, and the pain never seemed to fully subside, but there was a resilience in her that none of us could ignore.

Each morning, I would wake up to find her lying quietly in bed, her eyes closed, but her chest rising and falling with a steady rhythm. It was a small comfort. And despite the exhaustion that clung to her every movement, Emily would still try to engage with us. She'd smile at Lily's drawings, even when she couldn't lift her head from the pillow. She would watch Lily play in the garden from her window, her gaze soft and full of love, as if she were silently cheering her on, always present, even when she wasn't physically there.

There were still hard days, of course—days when Emily could barely speak, let alone sit up. But even on those days, her spirit never seemed to waver. She held onto something that kept her going, some invisible thread that tied her to this world, to us. I couldn't explain it, but I felt it, too.

One day, when the morning sun shone through the curtains, and the air was crisp with the promise of spring, something shifted. Emily had been sleeping for most of the morning, her face pale but peaceful, her hand resting gently in mine. Lily was in the living room, playing with her toys, creating her own little world. I sat by Emily's side, trying to focus on the moments we had together, but there was a nagging feeling deep inside me that something was different today.

Then, slowly, Emily's eyelids fluttered, and she woke up, her gaze unfocused at first. I held my breath, unsure if this was another of the difficult days or if there was something else at play. But as she looked up at me, her eyes clearing, I saw it—an undeniable spark.

"I'm... I'm not giving up yet," she whispered, her voice weak but strong at the same time. "I'm not ready. Not yet."

My heart swelled with a mixture of relief and disbelief. Emily had always been so strong, but this—this was something else entirely. She had been through so much, and yet here she was, fighting with every ounce of energy she had left.

Tears welled up in my eyes, but this time, they weren't tears of fear. They were tears of hope, of a future that suddenly seemed a little brighter. "You don't have to be ready yet, Emily. You've still got us. We're here. Lily's here."

She smiled faintly, and it was the first real smile I had seen in days. "I know. I just... I just need to get through this. I need to be here for Lily. For you. I need to see her grow up."

Her words hit me like a punch to the gut. She wasn't just fighting for herself. She was fighting for us. For Lily's future. For the life she had built with me.

It wasn't an easy road ahead. Emily still had her moments of weakness—there were still days when she could barely get out of bed, and the pain seemed unbearable. But that quiet determination in her eyes never wavered. It was as if something deep within her had shifted. She wasn't just passively waiting for the treatment to work. She was actively fighting, every single day.

We continued with the treatments, and with each passing day, Emily grew stronger. It was slow progress, but it was progress nonetheless. Her appetite began to return, and she could sit up for longer periods. There were even moments when she laughed—really laughed—at one of Lily's jokes or a silly story I told her. It was a sound I had almost forgotten, but one that filled our home with light and warmth again.

Lily, too, noticed the change. She began to spend more time with Emily, telling her about her adventures in the garden, showing her the flowers she'd picked, and asking her to help with the drawings she was making. Emily couldn't always keep up, but just the act of being there, listening, smiling when she could—it was everything. It was enough.

One afternoon, we sat together in the garden. Emily, wrapped in a soft blanket, her hand gently resting on mine, and Lily running around, chasing butterflies. The air was warm, and there was a sweetness to the moment that felt almost surreal. It was as if, for a few hours, time stood still, and we were able to live in the present, away from the worries of the future.

Emily watched Lily with such love, her eyes following her every move. "She's going to be okay, you know," Emily said softly, as though speaking to herself. "You're going to teach her everything, just like we promised."

I nodded, the lump in my throat almost choking me. "I will. I'll make sure she remembers everything you were—how much you loved her."

Emily squeezed my hand. "She already knows, in her heart. She's strong, just like you."

We sat there for a while, in silence, taking it all in. The garden, the light, the sound of Lily's laughter—it was more than just a peaceful moment. It felt like a victory. A victory over the fear and uncertainty that had threatened to take everything away.

There were still tough days ahead, of course. We all knew that. But in that moment, I realized something: Emily wasn't just fighting for herself—she was fighting for the future we could still have. She was fighting for our family, for the love that had always been at the center of everything.

And I knew, with all my heart, that as long as we had each other, we would continue to fight. Together.

No matter what came next.

# VIII

# The Final Goodbye

The days that followed felt like an endless stretch of time, each one heavier than the last. Emily had fought so hard—longer than anyone expected—clinging to the hope that maybe, just maybe, she could overcome this cruel disease. But no matter how much she fought, no matter how much strength she summoned from somewhere deep inside her, the cancer had spread too far. We had all known, deep down, that this battle would be one we couldn't win.

I watched as Emily's condition deteriorated in the final weeks. Her once vibrant spirit—her strength, her laughter, her fierce love—slowly faded, leaving behind a shell of the woman I had known. Her body became frail, the chemotherapy's toll evident in the way her skin stretched over her bones, her eyes darkened with exhaustion. And yet, even as her body weakened, her mind stayed sharp, her love for Lily and me still burning brightly.

But the truth was undeniable now. She was slipping away.

One evening, as I sat next to Emily's bed, holding her hand, I could feel the weight of it all pressing in on me. I could see the pain in her eyes, and I could feel her struggle to keep fighting, to keep holding on. But I also saw something else—a quiet resignation. As much as she wanted to stay, as much as she loved us, she was running out of time.

Her voice was faint, barely a whisper, when she finally spoke. "I... I don't think I can do this anymore," she said, her eyes gazing up at me. "I'm tired, love. So tired."

Tears welled up in my eyes, but I fought them back, trying to keep my voice steady. "No, Emily, you're not tired. You're just... you're just resting, okay? You've been through so much, but you're still here. And we're still here. You're not alone."

She gave me a weak smile, but it didn't quite reach her eyes. "I know. I know you'll take care of Lily. You'll make sure she remembers me. You'll tell her the stories. And you'll be strong for her... because she needs you."

The words hit me like a punch to the chest. I didn't want to think about a future without her, without her warmth, her love, the way she had been the heart of everything we had. "Emily, I can't do this without you. I need you. Lily needs you."

Her grip on my hand tightened for just a moment, and she blinked back the tears that had gathered in her eyes. "I'll always be with you. In your heart. In Lily's heart. I promise. I won't really be gone. I'll be with you, always."

But I knew what she meant. She was telling me goodbye.

I nodded, my chest tight with the weight of her words. "I promise, Emily. I'll keep you in my heart, always. I'll never forget. I love you so much."

She closed her eyes then, and for a moment, I thought she might drift off to sleep. But when she opened them again, they seemed to linger on me, as though trying to memorize my face one last time. And I tried to memorize hers, too—the soft curve of her cheek, the way her hair lay across the pillow, the way her eyes still held so much love for me.

"Lily... make sure she's okay," Emily whispered, her voice so faint I could barely hear it. "Promise me."

"I promise," I choked out, the words thick in my throat.

And just like that, Emily took one last breath, and her hand went limp in mine.

Time seemed to stop. The world outside of that room felt miles away, as though I were suddenly living in a different universe. The sound of the machines that had once beeped steadily now felt empty, hollow. My heart, shattered into a million pieces, struggled to find its rhythm, and for a long time, I didn't know how to breathe.

Lily came running into the room, her small voice full of innocence. "Mommy?" she asked, her face full of hope. "Is Mommy awake? Can we play?"

I turned to look at her, and for a moment, I couldn't speak. How could I explain to her what had just happened? How could I tell our little girl that her mother—her beautiful, strong, loving mother—was gone?

Lily's face crumpled as she saw the look on my face, the tears in my eyes. "Daddy? What's wrong?"

I knelt down in front of her, my heart breaking into a thousand jagged pieces as I held her close. "Mommy's gone, sweetie," I whispered, the words barely leaving my mouth as I held back the sobs. "Mommy... she had to go. She's in a better place now."

Lily's tiny hands grasped my shirt, and for a moment, she was silent, the weight of my words sinking in. Then, quietly, she whispered, "Is she coming back?"

I shook my head, my own tears falling freely now. "No, Lily. She's not coming back. But she'll always be with us. In our hearts. Forever."

I held her tightly, feeling the weight of my promise. Emily's love would live on in both of us—her laughter, her warmth, her wisdom—and somehow, I would carry it, and carry her, through the rest of our lives.

In the days that followed, the house was filled with an aching quiet. The laughter we once shared felt like a distant memory, replaced by the silence of loss. But even in that silence, Emily's spirit lingered. The love she had for us, for Lily, was something that couldn't be extinguished.

And though the pain of losing her would never fully fade, I knew that I had to carry on. I had to be the one to raise Lily, to honor the memory of the woman who had given me everything. I would tell Lily about her mother—about how kind, how brave, how strong Emily had been. I would make sure she knew how much her mommy had loved her, how proud she would always be of the woman Lily would become.

And in the quiet moments, when the world felt too heavy, I would close my eyes and remember Emily—the way she laughed, the way she loved, the way she fought. And I would carry that love with me, forever.

Because even though Emily was gone, her love would never leave.